If you haven't read Lexi's
side of the story yet,
please do that first!

Hello! The name's Melissa!
My middle name is Jan.
I love learning science,
And I play in the school band.

We were laughing during lunch,
Me and Lexi always do.
Swirling her carrot around she said,
"Who packed that UNHEALTHY lunch for you?"

It was time for recess and as always,
Lexi decided we'd play school.
She said, "You be the student, ask me this, then that.
Don't forget, I make the rules."

I stumbled in the halls,
And accidentally stepped out of line.
Lexi yelled, "I'M in front, Meliss.
EVERYONE, STAY BEHIND."

It was math time when Lexi said,
"That answer is VERY wrong."
I felt embarrassed, but she smiled at me,
Because the teacher was coming along.

The teacher said, "Choose your partners!"
It was time to work in pairs.
Russ said, "Will you be my partner?"
I would've said yes, but I felt scared.

Lexi grabbed my arm and said,
You can ONLY work with me.
She always makes me feel so sad,
It doesn't seem fair, you see?

I think it's time to let someone know,
About the way she makes me feel.
I think an adult will be able to help.
My feelings are feeling quite real.

Now that you've heard BOTH sides,
It's time to TALK them through.
It's so important to REFLECT.
What kind of friend are YOU?

Prompts for discussion:

1. At what point(s) did Lexi make a mistake in being a good friend?
2. At what point(s) do you think Lexi's word choices may have weakened her friendship with Melissa?
3. What are some things that Lexi can work on to become a better friend?
4. Have you ever made a mistake in being a good friend?
5. Has a friend ever made you feel bad? Did you let someone know?
6. What can you do to make sure that others are being treated right?
7. Can you create an ending to this story that would strengthen Lexi and Melissa's friendship?

Some tips for being a good friend and keeping your friends:

1. Be an **honest** friend - if you are bothered by something your friend does, let them know in a kind way.
2. Be a **helpful** friend - if your friend is struggling, don't make them feel bad about it. Meet them where they are and help them rise up. Rise up together.
3. Be a good **listener** - if your friend is being honest or opening up about something, just listen. You don't always have to fix their problems, you don't have to have the answers. Sometimes just offering our ears is enough.
4. Be a **positive** friend - encourage your friends, find things you admire in your friends, and let them know.
5. Be **receptive and compassionate** - if your friend seems uncomfortable or sad, acknowledge it. Offer words of comfort. Don't let them feel alone.
6. Be **empathetic** and take their **perspective** - show that you care about your friends and what they are experiencing in their lives. Ask questions to better understand where they are coming from and to understand why they feel the way they do about things - good or bad.
7. Be a friend who is **aware** - self-awareness helps us to understand ourselves. Strengthening our self-awareness is achieved by recognizing our overall strengths and weaknesses, recognizing how we react and act in situations, and recognizing how our actions or words affect others. Being a friend with strong self-awareness can strengthen a friendship.

What to do if you find yourself in a tough situation with a friend:

1. Talk with a parent or teacher to plan out some ways you can offer a solution to the problem while being kind, yet assertive.

For example, Melissa might say to Lexi:
> "I also like playing the teacher, so maybe we can take turns. Since you were first to play teacher today, I would love to be the first to play teacher tomorrow."

> "Maybe tomorrow, me, you and Russ can work in a group of three. He's really nice and I think we'll all work well together."

2. Talk with a parent or teacher to plan out how you can set boundaries and expectations.

For example, Melissa might say to Lexi:
> "I feel uncomfortable when you raise your voice at me, whether we are alone or in front of other people. If you do that again, I will have to ask an adult for help."

3. Talk with a parent or teacher to plan out how you can use your words to share how you are feeling.

For example, Melissa might say to Lexi:
> "It is hurtful when you make comments about what I am eating at lunch. It makes me sad. Just because my lunch doesn't look the same as yours, doesn't mean it isn't good."

> "I am so glad that we are friends. It made me uncomfortable when you suggested that I couldn't work with Russ on the class assignment. If I work with someone else, it doesn't mean that I will be any less of your friend than I am now."

Now CLOSE the book and
FLIP it over to hear
Melissa's side of the story.

The end of the day came so fast!
"What a good day, right, Meliss?
Mom's here to pick me up, bye!"
And I blew Meliss a kiss.

It's partner time and as always,
Me and Meliss are a pair.
Our friend Russ asked to work with Meliss,
Oh, I know she wouldn't dare!

Back to learning!
Melissa NEEDS my help during math.
"Meliss, I'll help you, I have an A+,
You can even ask Miss McGrath."

Recess is over, but it's okay,
I was chosen to lead the line!
It's finally here! The day has come!
"EVERYONE! STAY BEHIND!"

Recess is here! "Come on Meliss,
It's time to go outside.
Let's play school. I'll be the teacher.
You'll be Teacher if there's time."

It was lunchtime when I asked Meliss,
"What did you bring for lunch?"
My mom ALWAYS packs me healthy food,
Just hear my carrots crunch.

Here's my best friend Melissa,
I call her Meliss for short.
If I have a bad day, or even a good one,
She's right there for support.

Good morning school! Good morning friends!
My name is Lexi Drew.
I love my best friend Melissa,
And I LOVE love love love school.

I dedicate this book to Vanessa Anne, Olivia Belle, Michaela Jennie, Elizabeth Julia, Daniela Reese, Cristian Xavier, and Sofia Jo.

Always be **mindful** of your actions,
communicate how you are feeling,
listen to others,
reflect on how you can be better,
be **willing to change**,
and always **love** each other.

FOR MORE INFORMATION ABOUT THE AUTHOR AND SERIES VISIT:

Instagram: @juliefragnito.author | Facebook: Julie Fragnito, SEL Children's Book Author, M. Ed.

Printed in the United States of America

ISBN: 9781737086604

A TALE OF TWO STORIES:

Bully-ve In Yourself

(BELIEVE IN YOURSELF)

BY, JULIE FRAGNITO